Animal Skeletons

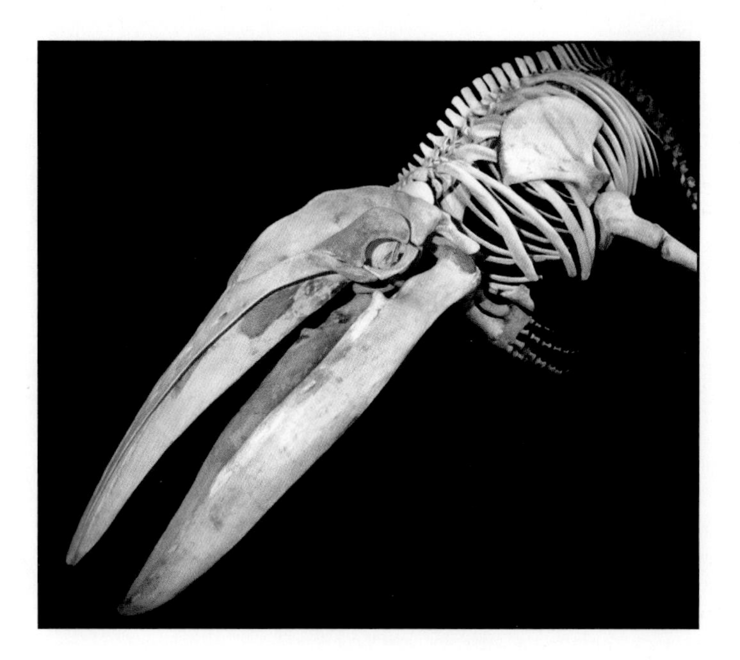

Written by Brylee Gibson

Here is a dog.
Look at the legs.

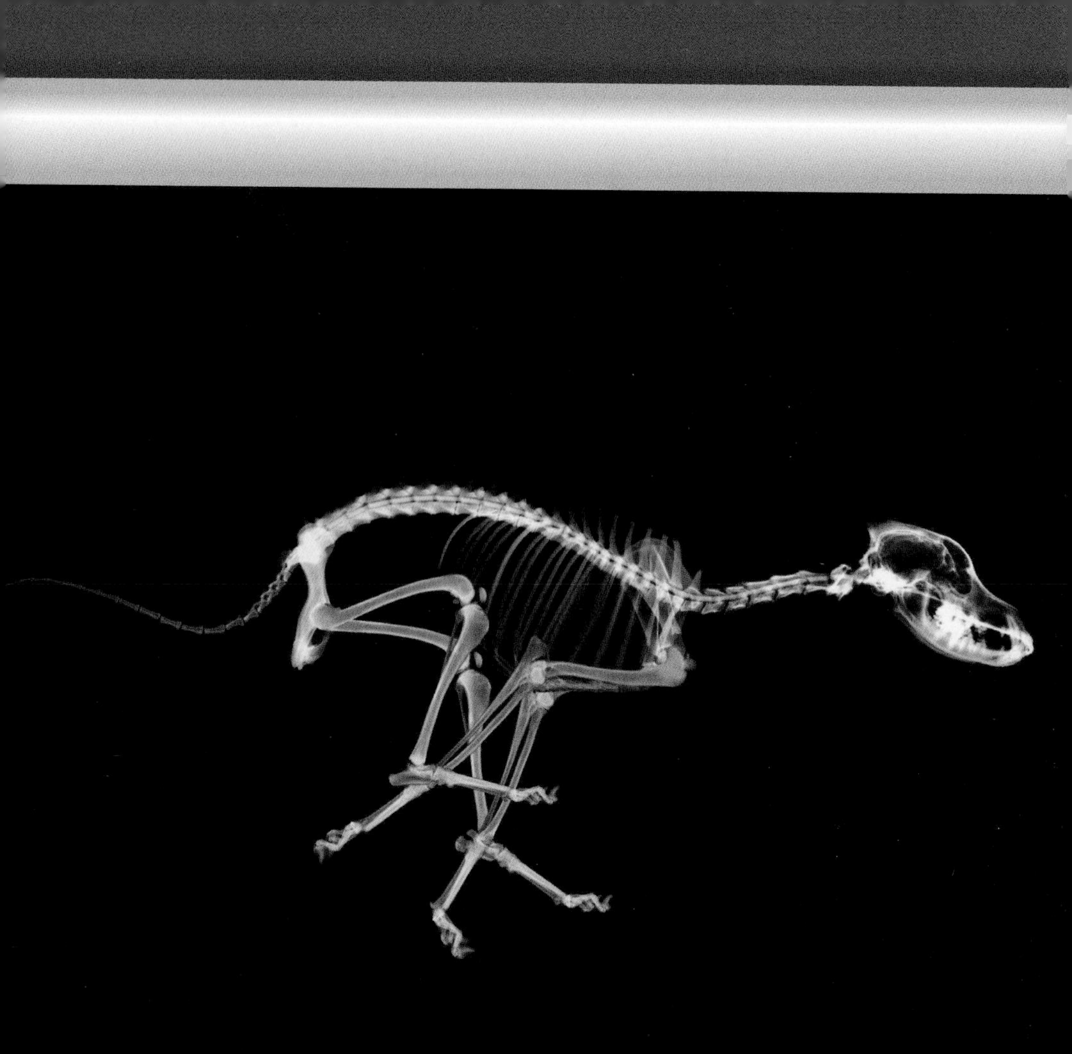

Here is the skeleton.
You can see the legs.

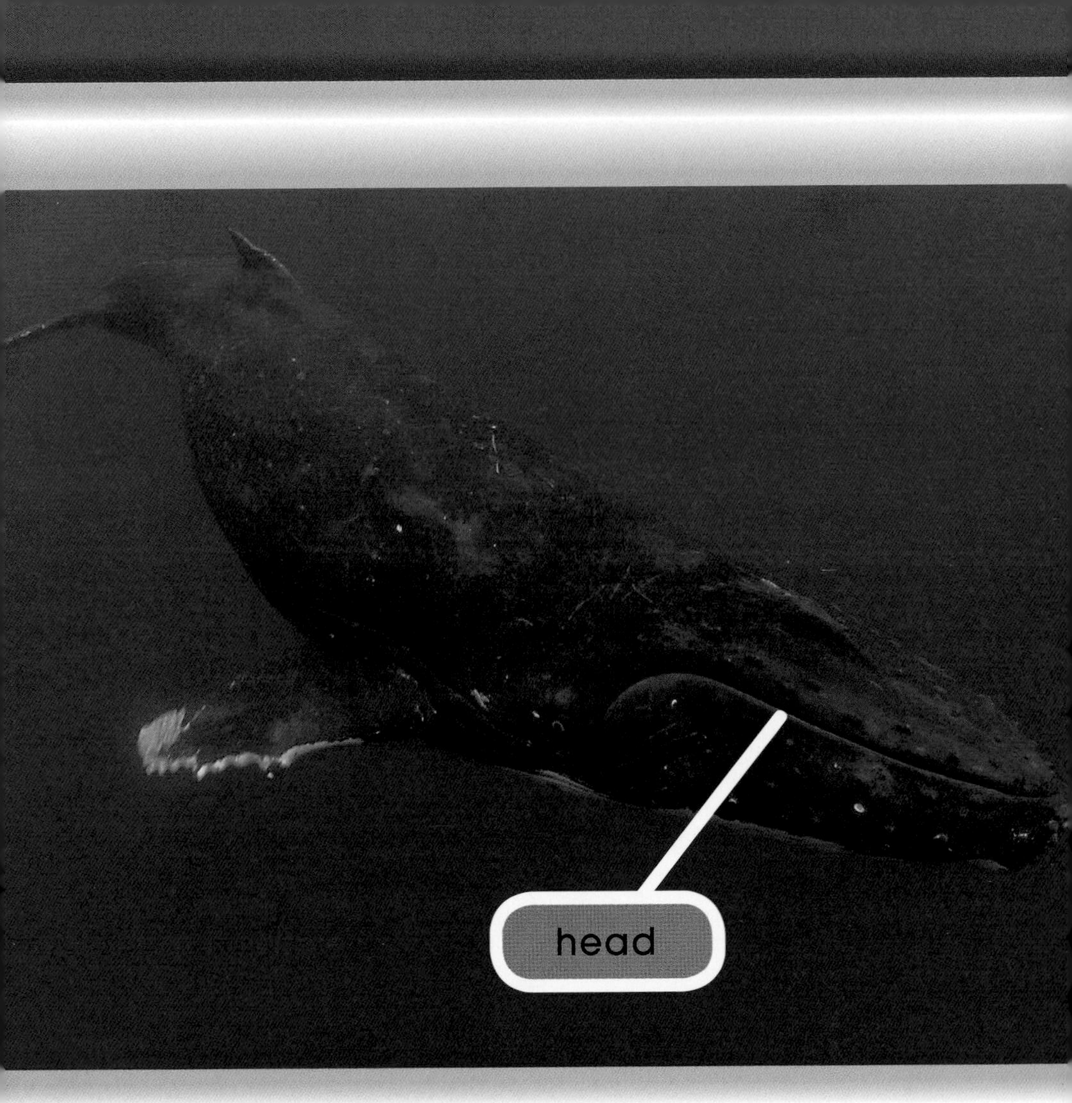

Here is a whale.
Look at the head.

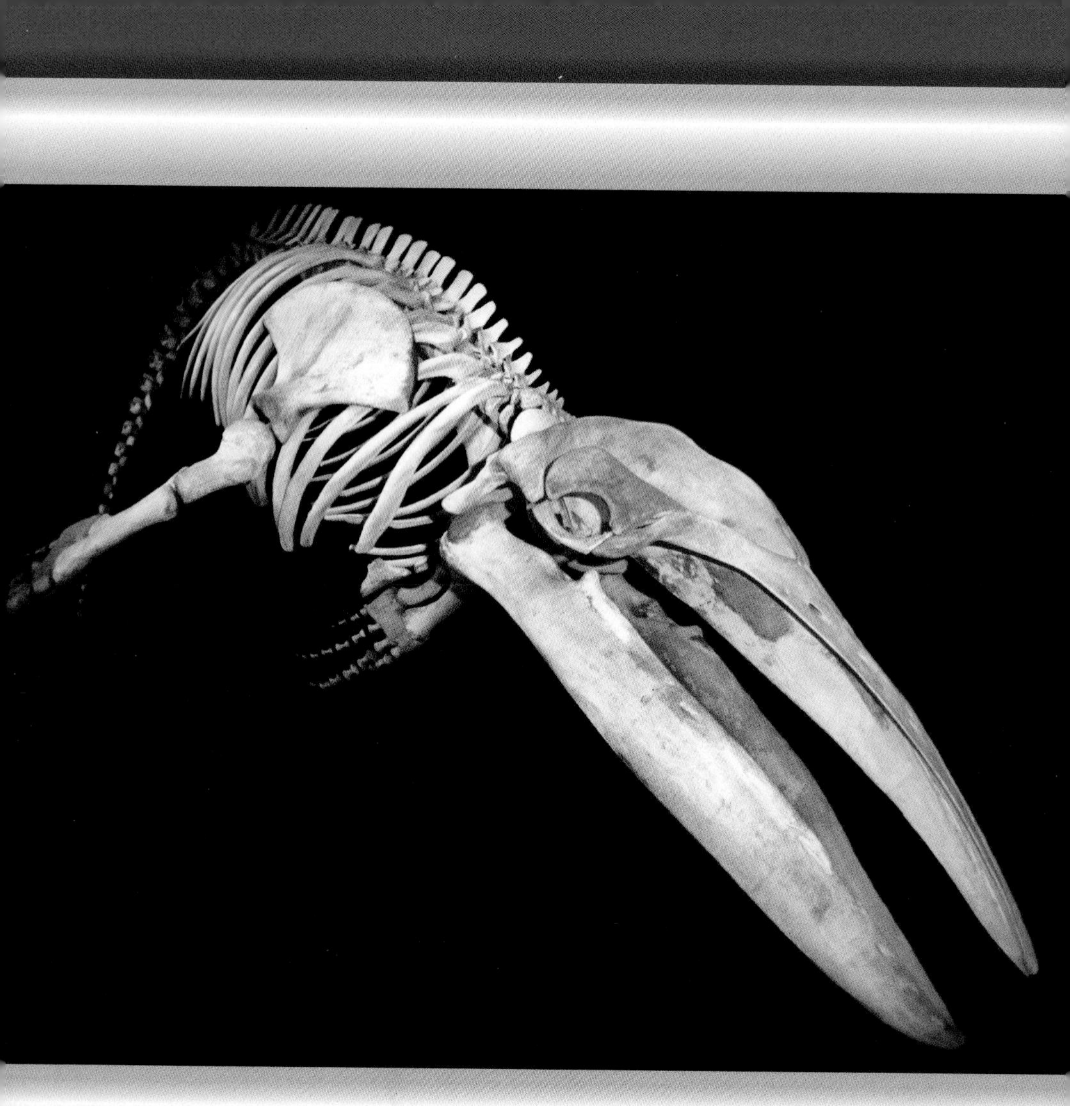

Here is the skeleton.
You can see the head.

Here is a bat.
Look at the wings.

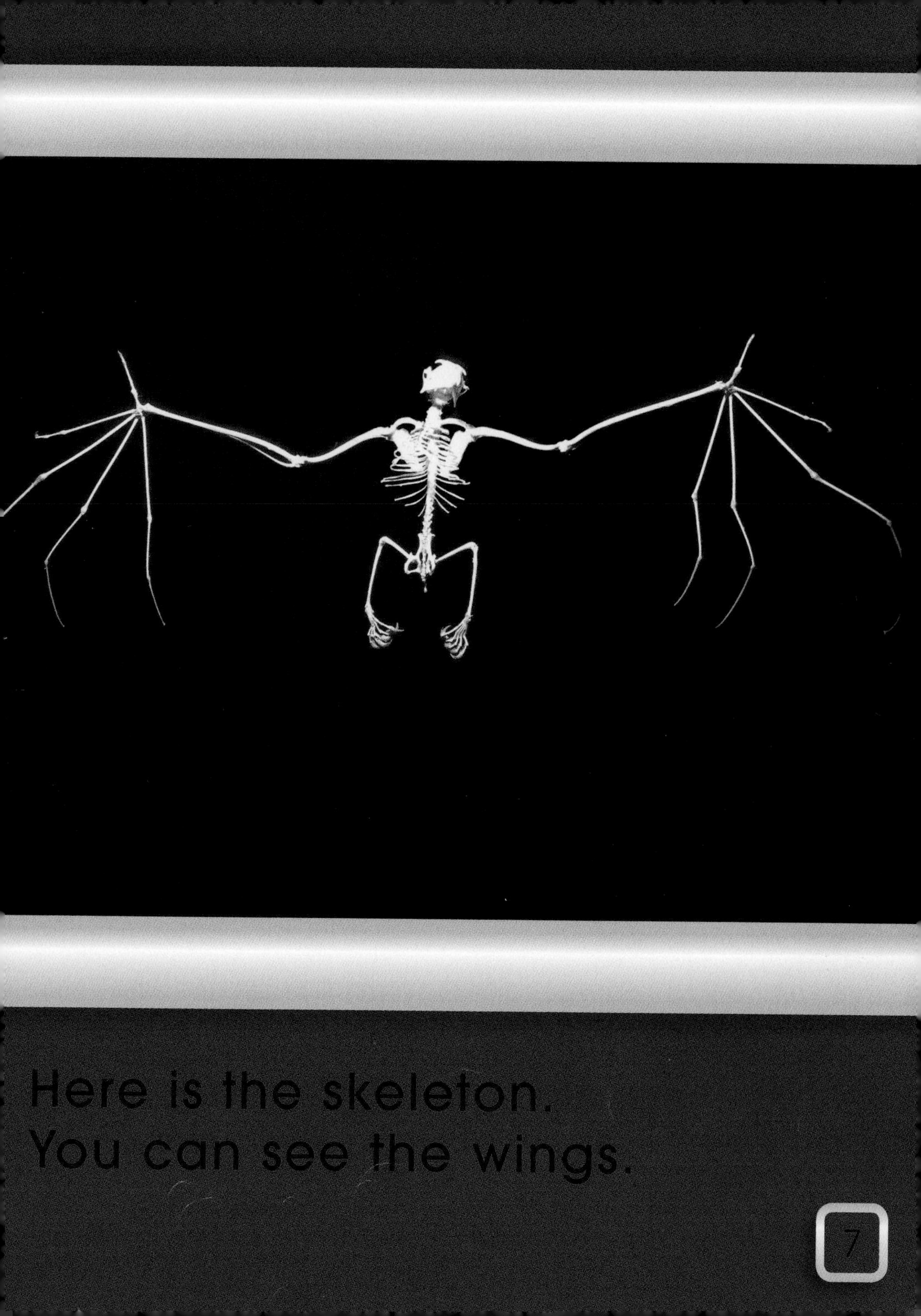

Here is the skeleton.
You can see the wings.

Here is a frog.
Look at the toes.

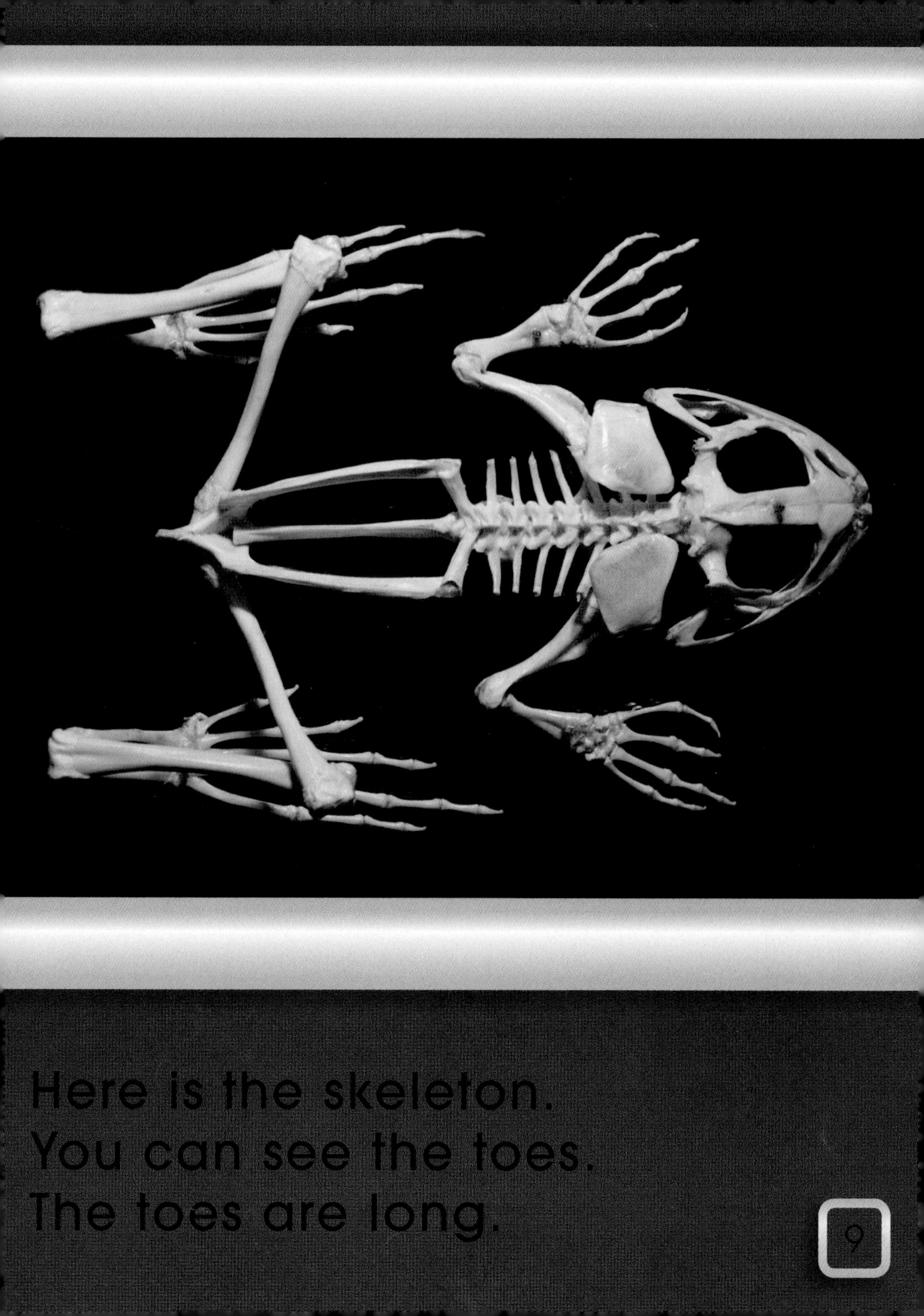

Here is the skeleton.
You can see the toes.
The toes are long.

Here is a monkey.
Look at the tail.

Look at the skeleton.
You can see the tail.
The tail is long.

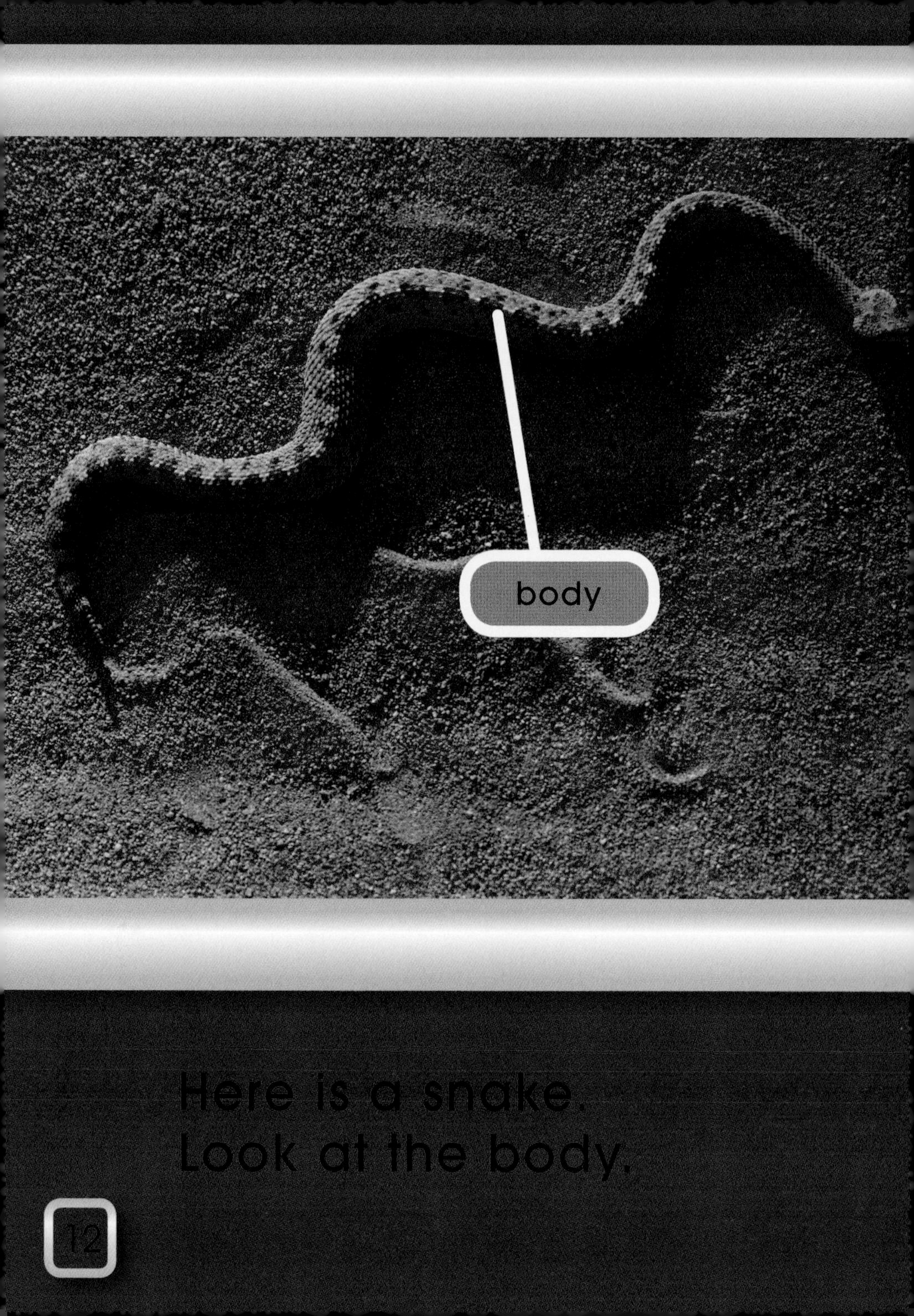

Here is a snake.
Look at the body.

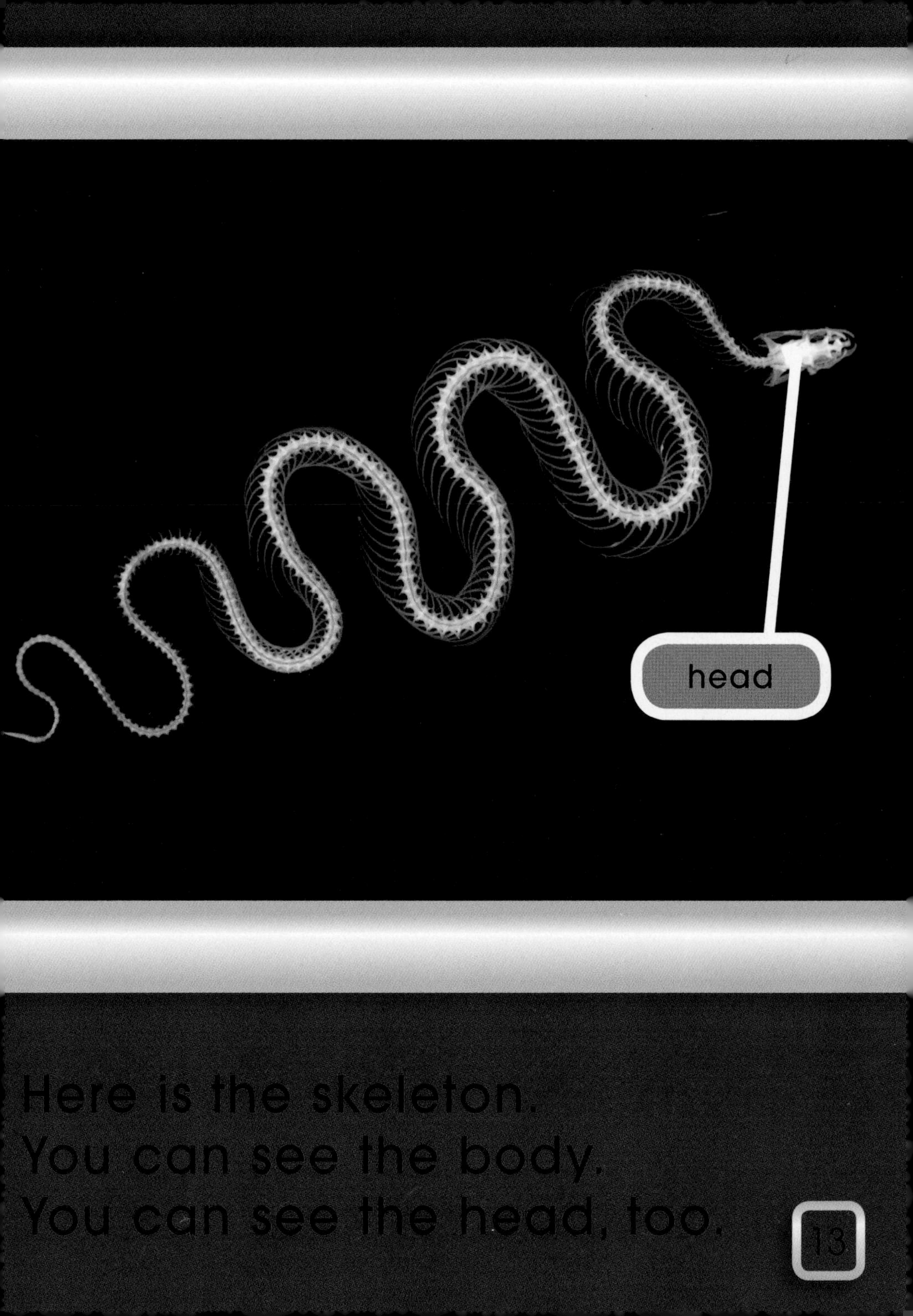

Here is the skeleton.
You can see the body.
You can see the head, too.

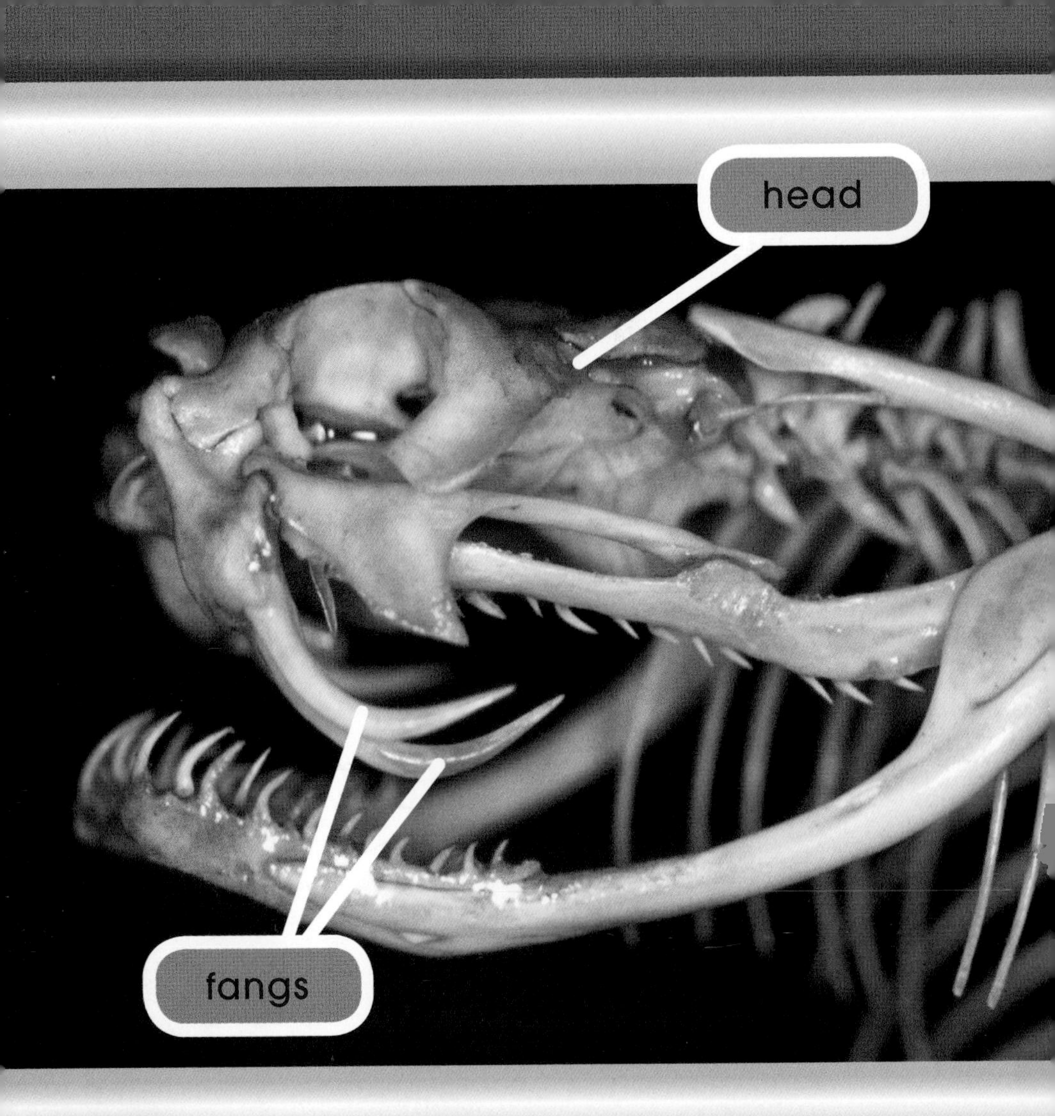

Look at the skeleton.
You can see the head.
You can see the fangs, too.

Index

Guide Notes

Title: Animal Skeletons
Stage: Early (1) – Red

Genre: Nonfiction
Approach: Guided Reading
Processes: Thinking Critically, Exploring Language, Processing Information
Written and Visual Focus: Photographs, Index, Labels

Thinking Critically

(sample questions)

- Look at the title and read it to the children.
- Tell them that this book is about some animal skeletons
  Clarify the meaning of skeletons and ask children what they know about skeletons.
  Focus the children's attention on the index. Ask: "What are you going to find out about in this book?"
- If you want to find out about the skeleton of a dog, which pages would you look on?
- If you want to find out about the skeleton of the frog, which pages would you look on?
- Why do you think some animals need to have a skeleton?
- How can you tell the animal by looking at the skeleton?

Exploring Language

Terminology

Title, cover, author, photographs, photographers

Vocabulary

Interest words: skeleton, head, wings, toes, fangs, tail
High-frequency word: too

Print Conventions

Capital letter for sentence beginnings, periods, comma, exclamation mark